STEFAN & OLGA

STORY AND PICTURES BY **BETSY DAY**

Dial Books for Young Readers New York

Published by Dial Books for Young Readers • A Division of Penguin Books USA Inc.
375 Hudson Street • New York, New York 10014

Printed in Hong Kong by South China Printing Company (1988) Limited
First Edition
W
1 3 5 7 9 10 8 6 4 2

Library of Congress Cataloging in Publication Data
Day, Betsy. Stefan and Olga.
Summary: A disastrous harvest forces Stefan to sell his beloved pet goose
Olga, but a practical application of his musical talent saves the day.
[1. Geese—Fiction. 2. Farm life—Fiction. 3. Musicians—Fiction] I. Title.
PZ7.D3293St 1991   [E]   89-23647
ISBN 0-8037-0816-5
ISBN 0-8037-0817-3 (lib. bdg.)

The art for this book was created using watercolor and pencil. It was then
color-separated and reproduced as red, blue, yellow, and black halftones.

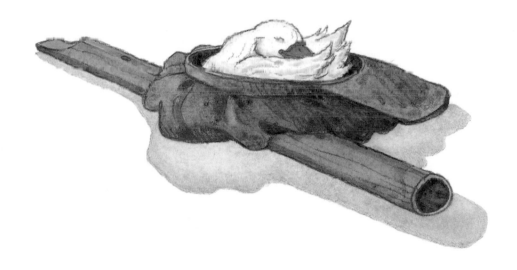

Stefan and Olga lived in a cozy house on a small farm. Every day Olga helped Stefan carry water and gather vegetables for their supper. Huffing and puffing while they worked, Stefan would tell Olga stories of times gone by.

"I remember when I first found you. You were a scrawny, awkward gosling. And now look at you—strong, healthy, and beautiful!"

After supper, night after night, they sat outside and watched the sun set. Stefan rocked in his chair and played soft, sweet music on the flute he had whittled. Olga loved Stefan's music so much that sometimes she would raise her beak, let out a whistle, and dance as gracefully as any ballerina.

But the seasons changed and harvesttime came as leaves fell from the trees. Stefan and Olga loaded baskets with the summer's crops.

But something was wrong. Half the baskets still lay empty. "We should have had more rain, my dear Olga," Stefan said as he threw most of the dried and dead vegetables into the garbage heap. "What are we going to sell . . . ?"

Then Stefan remembered the old silver candlestick on the table. Perhaps this would be the answer. With high hopes he patted Olga goodbye and set off to sell his treasure.

The kind neighbor down the road listened sympathetically and paid more than the candlestick was worth. But it was still not enough money to keep both of them through the winter.

Stefan laid the coins out on the table and shook his head. There was nothing left to sell. Stefan knew what he had to do.

That night there was no soft music, no stories. Stefan just sat inside and stared at the fire. Olga ruffled her feathers worriedly.

The next morning Stefan woke early and used the last of their supplies to cook all of Olga's favorite breakfast treats. Olga stood on her chair and honked merrily, trying to get Stefan to smile. But even bright music and the smell of blueberry griddlecakes were not enough.

Stefan solemnly watched Olga eat and when she was done he kneeled by her chair.

"Olga, my pet, I have something to tell you." Olga looked up. "At the market today I will have to find someone else to take care of you. I cannot afford to feed even one of us. One day I hope you will forgive me."

So together they walked sadly to town, where many people were buying and selling their wares. It wasn't long before a burly man approached them.

"Sir," said the burly man to Stefan, "are you interested in selling that goose? I'd be willing to pay a fair price."

Stefan and the man haggled for a long time. Finally Stefan said, as if from far away, "I'm sorry, Olga. I will miss you, but you will be taken care of. I made sure of that." He kissed the top of her head and disappeared into the crowd.

As soon as Stefan was out of sight, the burly man yelled, "*MOVE, GOOSE, MOVE!!!*"

Olga was startled. No one had ever talked to her like that before. Her new owner dragged her from one booth to another while he bartered and barked at everyone. Far off Olga heard the haunting music of a flute, and she raised her beak, but couldn't choke out a sound.

Aimlessly Stefan wandered through the crowd, playing his flute and trying to find some comfort in the familiar tunes. People started to gather and listen to his somber melodies, but he didn't notice them. When Stefan finally did look up, he was startled to see so many faces looking at him. Some of the people began to clap; some tossed coins at his feet; others danced.

Oh my, Stefan thought. All this for a simple tune.

Then it occurred to him. This is how I can get Olga back! Again he began to play. This time it was a much happier tune, which brought more people and more good fortune.

Stefan quickly gathered the money he had earned, excused himself from the jubilant crowd, and ran back to where he had last seen Olga.

But she wasn't there.

Stefan hurried around and around the square, asking anyone who would listen, but no one had seen her. The crowd began to thin. Vendors packed up their carts to go home. And Stefan's hopes faded.

Suddenly a tremendous racket erupted on a side street. There was Olga being pushed into a crowded cart over the oinking, honking, and braying protests of other animals.

"Stop!" Stefan shouted. "Stop! I've come to buy back my Olga!"

The burly man grinned evilly. "Why should I sell her back to you?" he asked. "Some butcher will pay plenty for this succulent goose."

The thought chilled Stefan's heart. But the burly man just snickered and drove away.

Olga squeezed past the noisy animals to where a crack opened in the wagon's side. Far away she could see Stefan still running after them. Suddenly Olga had an idea.

She picked her spot, closed her eyes, and jabbed her beak sharply into the hindquarters of the donkey. With a loud, pain-filled wheeze the donkey kicked and bucked at the gate.

"What's going on back there?" boomed the burly man, jumping from his seat. "Stop it! Stop it!"

But the donkey kept kicking frantically. And with one splintering crack the rickety gate fell to pieces.

Olga honked and flapped her wings at the other animals. Off they went, quacking and squealing, leaving behind a cloud of dust, fur, and feathers.

Above all the noise you could hear the burly man hollering for the animals to come back, as they disappeared over a hill.

By this time Stefan had caught up to them.

"Olga, my Olga," he said, huffing and puffing. "I was so afraid I would never see you again. I hope you will forgive an old man for making such a terrible mistake."

Olga nuzzled his neck.

"Let's go home now, huh, Olga? I think you might have a story or two for me this time." Before they left, Stefan carefully put the pouch of money on top of the demolished cart.

As the two of them continued on their way, Stefan happily played his flute while Olga danced and whistled close by his side.